CUENTO DE LUZ

*With my admiration and thanks to the wise naturalist Joaquín Araújo
and all those like him who love and care for the forests.*
—Susana Rosique

This book is printed on **Stone Paper** that is **Silver Cradle to Cradle Certified®**.

Cradle to Cradle™ is one of the most demanding ecological certification systems, awarded to products that have been conceived and designed in an ecologically intelligent way.

Cuento de Luz™ became a **Certified B Corporation** in 2015. The prestigious certification is awarded to companies that use the power of business to solve social and environmental problems and meet higher standards of social and environmental performance, transparency, and accountability.

Agreement Under the Stars
Text and illustrations © 2024 by Susana Rosique
© 2024 Cuento de Luz SL
Poniente 92 | Pozuelo de Alarcón | 28223 | Madrid | Spain
www.cuentodeluz.com
Original title in Spanish: *Acuerdo bajo las estrellas*
English translation by Jon Brokenbrow
ISBN: 978-84-19464-82-8
1st printing, Legal Deposit Spain: M-2331-2024
Printed in PRC by Shanghai Cheng Printing Company, February 2024, print number 1901-21

Agreement
Under the Stars

By Susana Rosique

There once was a time when the forest
was so wide it seemed to go on forever.
The animals lived together in peace and harmony,
without disturbing each other.

But little by little, day by day,
the outside world grew around them,
and the forest began to get smaller and smaller.

That was when the problems began . . .

"We can't go on
like this . . ."

There wasn't as much space as there used to be. An emergency committee came up with a solution: They couldn't all use the space at the same time anymore. Some animals would be active during the day and sleep at night, while others would come out at night and sleep during the day.

"What a great idea!" they all said.

But nobody volunteered to be on the night shift. And so, the committee selected those who'd be the night creatures, the heroes who would live out their lives exiled in the shadows for the common good.

"BECAUSE WE'RE HIDEOUS!

They're shoving us into the darkness so they don't have to see us anymore!"

"Because we're handsome?"

Chirp

Chirp

Chirp

The animals looked at each other.

They weren't majestic or cute.
They didn't have silky skin or bright feathers.
They didn't have beautiful voices.
They didn't look graceful when they walked.

For the first time ever, they felt grotesque, ugly,
and drab. And from that night on, they hid in
the darkness so they couldn't be seen.

One night, a poacher came into the forest
and set out a lot of traps.

Owl hooted mournfully all night until dawn,
in hopes of warning all the animals.

The night creatures were saved, but the day creatures ignored the warning, and some of them were caught in the traps.

At nightfall, when Toad came out in search of his breakfast, he heard a tremendous racket. Finch and Rabbit were yelling. They were trapped in cages. Toad looked at them and opened his enormous mouth. With his long, sticky tongue . . .

. . . he tore the doors off the cages and set them free.

Bat and Hedgehog found Deer caught in a snare. Hedgehog rolled himself into a spiky ball, while Bat fluttered around, biting at the trap with his sharp little teeth.

Together, they set Deer free.

When Mole found Fox howling noisily, with her
beautiful tail caught in the trap he got to work.
Using his strong, sharp claws, he set her free.

As grateful as they were ashamed, all the members of the committee asked the night creatures if they'd like to go back to living during the daytime. They'd find another solution to the lack of space. But the night creatures kindly refused the invitation; an agreement was an agreement, and it had to be respected.

And what's more . . .

They'd gotten used to the peace and quiet of the night.

They didn't crave frills or flattery.

Under the silver moonlight,

the world wasn't black or white;

there was room for all the shades of gray.

DID YOU KNOW . . . ?

Our forests are home to lots of different animals. The reason why there are daytime and nocturnal animals isn't exactly the way we've told it in this story. But it's a fact that there are fewer and fewer forests on our planet. Deforestation, the uncontrolled chopping down of trees, forest fires, the extraction of resources from the earth, and large-scale construction have all caused, in just a short space of time, the disappearance of one-third of our forests.

We know that forests, apart from being the home and refuge of living creatures, also store carbon and absorb polluting gases from the atmosphere, maintain the humidity of the environment, and protect the soil against landslides and desertification. If we care for them and manage them sustainably, we'll be looking after the planet and ourselves. There are plenty of things we can do to save them! To find out more and lend a hand, you can contact national or international associations, foundations, and organizations.

Cuento de Luz, the publisher of this book, has made a firm commitment to nature and sustainability with "ecopublishing": their books are printed on "stone paper," a special paper made of limestone, the most abundant material on Earth. This paper doesn't come from cutting down trees, doesn't use water, and doesn't need chemical products such as chlorine.

THINGS I CAN DO TO TAKE CARE OF THE FORESTS:

_____

_____

_____

_____

_____

_____

_____